# ANDREW FUSEK PETERS

# Breathe
# AND YOU DIE

from the author of Ravenwood

RIVETS

EDGE

Also by Andrew Fusek Peters:

*Ravenwood*

*Skateboard Detectives*

*The Glass Forest*

*Roar! Bull! Roar!*

*Falcon's Fury*

# ANDREW FUSEK PETERS

# Breathe
# AND YOU DIE

EDGE
FRANKLIN WATTS

LONDON•SYDNEY

First published in 2013
by Franklin Watts

Text © Andrew Fusek Peters 2013
Cover design by Peter Scoulding

Franklin Watts
338 Euston Road
London NW1 3BH

Franklin Watts Australia
Level 17/207 Kent Street
Sydney, NSW 2000

A CIP catalogue record for this book
is available from the British Library.

Slava Gerj/Shutterstock: front cover c.
Anna Kucherova/Shutterstock: front cover b.
lolloj/Shutterstock: front cover top.

(pb) ISBN: 978 1 4451 2313 4
(ebook) ISBN: 978 1 4451 2316 5
(Library ebook)0 ISBN: 978 1 4451 2578 7

1  3  5  7  9  10  8  6  4  2

Printed in Great Britain

Franklin Watts is a division of
Hachette Children's Books,
an Hachette UK company.
www.hachette.co.uk

*To my son Asa,*
*the original*
*Karate Kid!*

# Contents

# Chapter One

7PM

Matt woke up coughing. The
smell in his nose was rank, a mix
of rotten eggs and dead meat.
Where was he? And why did his
head hurt? He slowly opened his
eyes. Weird. He was lying on bare

floorboards in a room he'd never seen in his life. He still wore his school clothes, now scuffed and torn. If this was a dream, it was convincing.

Thick smoke hovered a few inches above his head. More of it poured in from a vent high in the ceiling. Here, down by the floor, the air was almost clear.

It didn't take a science degree to know the smoke was poison. If he sat up, and breathed it in, he'd be dead. Matt tried to think.

Last thing he remembered, he was leaving school late after his karate lesson. His *kata* had been good and the *sensei*, his teacher, was pleased with Matt's progress. What else? There'd been a van with tinted windows, slowing down alongside him. Then... nothing. Matt coughed again; he could feel the gas exploring his lungs, trying to shut him down for good.

It didn't make sense. He was an ordinary year 9 boy, who went to a boring school. A brown belt in *Shotokan* karate, even with a second stripe, was hardly a threat. Every second he lay there thinking, the smoke above his head grew thicker. He had to get out.

Apart from the bump on his head, he appeared to be in one piece. He crawled as close to the floor as possible towards the door. The room narrowed into a corridor. When he finally got to the end and reached up with his arm, the door was firmly locked and the letter box was nailed down. Who

would do this to him? It was mad!
He slid backwards. Maybe he'd
have better luck with the window.

Matt grabbed a deep lungful of
clean air and stood up, using both
arms to try and slide the window
open. The smoke made his eyes
smart. Why wouldn't it budge?
He looked again. Window lock.
Damn! Think, Matty. Think! Of
course — the dirty plastic chair
by the window. It had metal legs.
He knelt down to take another
breath and grabbed the chair,
swinging with all his might against

the glass. There was a satisfying crash and shards of glass flew everywhere. Smoke streamed out, the room cleared. The foul gas was gone and he was alive, though he wondered if the small amounts of gas he had breathed in would damage his lungs. He took a deep breath. Everything seemed to be working.

Matt ran to the window. The force of the chair had broken the window lock. He managed to wrench the frame open to look out. Though it was dusk already,

the streetlights showed where
he was — the top floor of the old
block in Hay Court that was due
for demolition. But who the hell
had brought him here?

His ears told him the answer.
There were footsteps on the stairs
outside. He knew they weren't
coming to see how he was. They'd
already tried to kill him once and
they weren't going to stop now.

# Chapter Two

**7.15PM**

Matt was trapped. He glanced towards the window, but the drop was thirteen floors. Any second and those people outside would be through the door. His sensei always said: "fast on your feet, quick in your head". Easy for the old man, teaching a bunch of teenagers and little kids.

Matt looked around the room for an escape, a cupboard to hide in. The room was bare, though the layout was odd, with high ceilings and a narrow corridor leading to the door. Matt felt his mind fire up. He'd beaten death once. Not bad for a year 9 pupil. Time to make it a habit. He ran towards the door, swivelled sideways and put his hands on the left-hand wall.

Keys were already in the lock, as Matt lifted his right foot and braced himself across the corridor. He heard a gruff voice from the other side of the door. "Check it out. If he's gone, Putenov won't be pleased!"

Matt's muscles complained as he slowly, too slowly, shuffled upwards towards the ceiling. All those hours of training paid off. It felt like levitation as he hovered close to the ceiling, every part of his body tense and taut.

The door slammed open and a
man ran in, black leather jacket,
jeans, slicked-back hair almost
hidden by the gas mask covering
his face. Amazingly, he passed
straight underneath Matt. Matt
tried to keep his breathing
shallow, but his heart raced and
his legs were already cramped.
The gun in the man's thick hand
didn't look like a toy. The man
ran to the window, paused to look
out, then swore under his breath.
As he turned, Matt tried to think
himself invisible.

The man sniffed once, then pulled his mask off and smiled. "Clever. I'll give you that. But do I look blind?" The gun motioned Matt to climb down.

Matt eased himself down, his whole body trembling. "Why do you want to kill me?"

"Don't take it personal, mate. You saw too much. We got big plans for tomorrow and don't want no hold-ups. Now, I'm gonna have to finish what I started."

Matt knew the man was without fear. Almost worthy of admiration. What had the founder of Shotokan said? "The ultimate aim of karate lies not in victory or defeat, but in the perfection of the character of the participant." Fat lot of good that would do now. All Matt had was a room, a chair by the window, a man with a weapon and his own instincts. He had to appear weak, to get the man off his guard.

"But I'm only a kid!" Matt cowered in fear.

"No. What you are is a glitch in our business. Once this silencer's screwed in, problem solved."

Matt had bought a couple of seconds. It was all he needed. Karate had been about theory. This was the real test.

The man's eyes went wide, as Matt leaped forward, landing on the chair. Kids were supposed to run away! The man's gun began to swing up. Too late. Matt sprang off the chair, using it as a platform to launch his body straight at his attacker. His right leg uncurled, then slammed straight into the man's chest.

It was a flying *Mae Geri* kick, executed perfectly. The man's gun flew from his fingers as the air was expelled from his lungs. All the force of Matt's anger propelled the man backwards straight through the open window. Gone. Thirteen floors and one second later, the man's scream was cut short by a sickening thump.

Matt should have felt relieved.

But he'd just killed a man and he wasn't out of trouble yet.

# Chapter Three

MOMENTS LATER

Matt ran down the street, trying
to ignore the pain in his right
foot. As night set in, a thin drizzle
made the pavement slippery.
He'd escaped by hiding in one of
the empty flats as the other man

had run past him. What could he do? He was about to skid round the corner that led home when instinct stopped him dead. A car was parked a few yards from his house. A figure flicked ash out of the car window then took a drag on a cigarette. The glow lit up the driver's face.

Damn! How had they found his house? Matt shrunk back into the shadows, turned round and sprinted off. What he didn't see was the figure climb out of the driver's seat and run straight towards the spot where Matt had been hiding.

Five minutes later, Matt was sure he'd got away. He slowed to a walk. Perhaps he was safe. He pulled out his mobile, tapping in the numbers, his eyes flicking behind him. Nothing, except a few people scurrying past the shuttered shops on their way home from work. He put the mobile to his ear.

"Leah, are you there? I think I'm in trouble."

"Course you are!" the voice of his best friend came back. "What's new?"

"No joking, girl. Someone tried to kill me, and..." As Matt walked slowly towards the park, he laid out the whole story. It seemed impossible. But a cut on his hand from the broken glass told him it was true.

"... And I think I killed one of them," Matt finished. He felt sick. In karate, the end goal was always freedom from violence.

"Listen. I don't know what to say but..." Leah paused. "It was you or him, right? And you, my friend, have kicked some proper ass!"

"Cheers, Leah." Matt was about to walk through the gate into the park. "But why me?"

"I don't know. Maybe it was that van you saw pulling into school after karate?"

"Dunno." Matt had only mentioned it in passing. A van dropping off some gas bottles at school. Then he remembered the guy in the van that had stared at him and...

"You heard one of them mention some guy Putenov?"

"Yeah."

"The master hacker will go to work and check it out! Stay safe and..."

Matt suddenly felt his shoulders gripped in a vice.

"Drop it, boy! Now!"

The phone clattered to the ground.

"You did my mate. Now I'm gonna do you!"

Matt could hardly move, as pain shot through his shoulders. The guy was strong, the park around them empty and dark. Even if he screamed, who would notice in this place? Any moment now, the grip would shift to his neck. One twist and it would break.

The man expected Matt to tense up. Matt did the opposite, letting his muscles go instantly floppy. It worked. For a split second, the fingers that clutched onto him became loose. Matt twisted to his right, easily breaking free. Forget the phone. Time to run.

This time, there was no easy escape. The man was equally fast. Each time Matt darted down another dark path, or circled round a set of looming bushes, he felt his pursuer's breath almost on his back — he was sticking like superglue!

Another park gate reared up. Matt dived through, not sure where he was, which way to go. Left, then right, then... The railway arch he'd ducked into had been bricked up. His direction was blocked. Dead end.

The man was so close behind that Matt could hear him swearing under his breath. Then the pause, as his pursuer also worked out there was nowhere to go. Matt had to think fast. So what if

it was a blank wall? His free-
runner mates saw obstacles as
a challenge. He'd gone out with
them a few times, tried out some
of the moves. But they did it for
kicks, filming them to upload and
get the credit they deserved. No
one was filming here. Oh well.
Nothing to lose.

Matt ran straight at the wall,
checking its height, knowing that
even the best free-runner would
never get up it. That wasn't his
plan. A couple of yards before
slamming into it, he leaped

upwards with his right foot forward. Speed was the key. And the wall now had to be thought of as flat. His foot made contact with the brickwork and he began to run up the wall. Two strides and he leant all his weight back until gravity kicked in and he was flipping backwards right over his astonished attacker.

The landing was messy, but it would do, as he thumped onto the ground and closed onto his attacker. Before the man could turn round, Matt aimed all his

anger and frustration into one
good kick between the guy's legs.

The man squealed, then
collapsed.

No time to admire the stunt
that had just saved his life. Matt
sprinted back towards the park.
He was amazed to find the phone
still there, even more amazed
that Leah was still on the line.

"Are you all right?"

"Spot of bother," Matt panted.

"Right. Interesting guy, your Putenov. Listen up."

# Chapter Four

ONE HOUR LATER
Matt and Leah crouched down
behind a bin, trying to keep to
the shadows. The building behind
the fence was dark.

"Why are we spying on our own

school?" Matt hissed.

Leah tapped her phone screen with a blur of fingers. "Told you. There ain't no network I can't crack."

"And?" said Matt. "I'm knackered, my hand hurts and I haven't eaten since lunch."

"It all makes sense," hissed Leah. "You saw a van delivering gas bottles. A few hours later, you're nearly dying from some kind of poison gas. Yeah?"

"I don't get it."

"Matty, your brain's stopped working. But listen, Radek Putenov is opening the new kitchen at the school tomorrow. Big donation and all that, helping pupils eat well. Typical millionaire. Not so typical, and harder to find out, is that he majored in biochemistry and all that dosh came from developing a lethal nerve gas for the Russians."

"So he's planning a terrorist attack?"

"No. It's all about revenge. One of his funders was Lebed, the banker. The name means swan in Russian. Turns out he swanned off with a few million in bribes and thought Putenov never knew."

"Hang on. I know that name. Tanya Lebed, the leggy black-haired girl in my tutor group."

"Stop going moony-eyed, Matty. She's so out of your league."

"Yeah, yeah."

"Point is, when Putenov does revenge, he does it big style."

Matt's mouth hung open. "Kill the kid. In fact, kill all the kids. Oh my God!"

"God's got nothing to do with it. Unless we do something, it's going to be a massacre."

"We should have rung the police."

"Really? 'Hello, Ms Policewoman. I just threw a man to his death. And by the way, our local

millionaire is planning to murder
a whole school tomorrow!' Yes, I
can see them believing that."

"So it's up to us then?"

"Unless you have any better
ideas."

"Actually, I do."

*    *    *

Twenty minutes later, Leah
sniffed the air in distaste as she
looked around.

"Is this your idea of breaking and entering?"

"Welcome to the world of the boys' loos!' Matt whispered. 'The smell's so bad, they always leave at least one window open."

"Too much detail!"

It was strange creeping through corridors normally thronging with pupils. Every shadow loomed, and Matt found it hard to breathe calmly. They crept into the main hall. At the far end, light leaked round the edges of metal shutters. There were muffled voices and the sound of hammering. They crouched down behind some stacked chairs.

"I still can't believe what he's going to do to all of us. It's insane!" Matt whispered.

A voice broke in. "Insane! Is that how you think of me?"

A man strode towards them. "No need to get up. You aren't going anywhere, after all." The man's voice was thick and nasal. He was surprisingly tall, and well-dressed in a grey suit and black tie.

"I am Putenov," he said.

Matt recognised the armed thug at his side.

"The mass-murderer!" Leah hissed through clenched teeth.

"Such an emotive term. It is merely business. If a friend steals from you, you have to show them the error of their ways."

"You what?" gasped Matt. "Kill a whole school, as well as his daughter? You're off your trolley!"

"I do love your quaint English phrases. In fact, I have never felt saner. Goodbye to both of you."

Putenov turned to the man at his side. "Misha, tie them and gag them. When we release the gas tomorrow, they shall breathe their last."

# Chapter Five

**8.30AM NEXT DAY**

Matt felt the boot in his ribs. The store cupboard wasn't the best place for a night's sleep. At least they were still alive, though his mum was probably worried sick.

"Wakey, wakey. My boss wants to give you a nice easy death," the man called Misha muttered. "In half an hour, during assembly, and after the stupid speeches, the kitchen will be opened and everyone will be served fresh croissants, coffee and... what was it... oh yeah, some nerve gas to wash it all down."

Matt could see the mask dangling from the man's belt. "And while my colleagues are having fun out there, I have to babysit you two until the gas has worked its way through the air vents. Then it's goodbye."

The man kneeled down by Matt, his beery breath almost making him gag. "But first... you dropped my mate to his death and possibly damaged my manhood. Now, 'cos there are teachers already out in the corridors, I'm going to leave your gag in while I break a few bones and teeth, nice and quiet like."

The man's fist raised up and Matt closed his eyes, waiting for the impact, the spurt of blood from his nose, the sharp crack of teeth rammed down his throat.

Instead, there was a groan of disbelief.

Matt opened his eyes. Misha still kneeled right in front of him, but something stuck out of his stomach. Leah was hopping on her tied-up legs, with the other end of a javelin held firmly in her hands. The thug slumped over, blood pooling round his knees.

A few minutes later they had managed to untie each other.

"Think he got the point?"

"That's sick!" Matt replied.

"Whatever. Do you think he's dead?" Leah whispered.

"Don't care," Matt replied. "Like that guy in the tower block, it was him or us."

"We should get everyone to evacuate."

"Not that easy. Putenov, or one of his men will simply set the gas off. We have to stop them. And before you ask, the police won't get here in time. We've only got minutes..."

They pushed the body under some gym mats and tidied themselves up. It was time for assembly.

# Chapter Six

**8.55**AM

Again the corridors were strangely
silent. Matt peered into the hall.
The whole school sat there, every
single teenager doing their best
to look bored while the teachers
patrolled. Putenov stood on stage

next to the head, talking quietly.

"What now?" said Leah.

"Kitchen," said Matt. "And fast. I overheard Putenov say that when the bell goes at nine, that's the signal to turn on the gas."

They ran round the corner and were going too fast to backtrack as the man guarding the kitchen doors clocked them. Already, he was reaching into his jacket, pulling out the machine pistol. Dimly, Matt's brain registered that guns like that didn't need to aim. The spray of bullets would cover a wide enough arc to punch holes the size of pound coins in their bodies. Without thinking, Matt opened his mouth and began to yell at the top of his voice. Leah caught on quick and joined in the shouting. The wall of sudden noise was enough to make the man pause.

Two crazy teenagers, sprinting straight towards him and mouthing the most disgusting swear words. Never mind. One pull of the trigger and they'd be out.

But Matt was already within striking distance. All he needed now was a launch pad. There was no convenient chair, but there were walls, and one of them would have to do. He leapt into the air, left foot skewing out to the side, knee bending as his foot impacted then sprung off the wall. His right knee was out even before the trigger finger could be pressed, slamming into the man's head with a meaty crack. The man crumpled, his gun clattering onto the lino floor.

Leah was already past him, pushing through the swing doors, shouting at the chef. "Don't turn on the gas!"

"What? But the croissants need fifteen minutes to cook!"

"It's all of us who will be cooked if you turn that on. The gas is poison. Trust me!"

The chef put his hands on his

hips. "Oh, ha ha! Get back to assembly. I'll have you reported for this!" he snarled.

Matt pushed open the door. In his hands, he held the machine pistol. It was aimed directly at the chef. "No lie, mister. Step away from the oven!"

*     *     *

It was over. Or rather, it wasn't. "Damn!" said Matt. "We forgot about Putenov." But by the time they had run back into the hall,

the whole place was in chaos
and the head was shouting at
everyone to calm down. By
Putenov's chair, there was a gas
mask. But the man himself was
gone.

*    *    *

3.15PM
Matt and Leah had never been
inside a police station before. At
least they weren't under arrest.
More importantly, the mugs of tea
brought into the interview room
were hot and sweet. Matt felt the

tiredness creeping up on him.

Inspector Weaver kept staring at them both as if they were some kind of new species. "It seems we and your school owe you our thanks."

"Yeah, well," Leah muttered.

"At first, we assumed it was a teenage prank gone too far."

"Really?" said Matt. "Not many teenagers larking about with deadly nerve gas..."

"I admit, the whole thing caught us on the hop. How Putenov hoped to get away with it, we don't know."

"But you did let him get away?" accused Leah.

"We have lookouts at every port and airport. He seems to have slipped the net."

"What about the guy who fell out of the tower block?" said Matt.

"And the one in the store

cupboard ... with the javelin?"
said Leah.

"I think self-defence covers all
bases. Some might even say you
both deserve a medal."

"Now you're talking! However,
I've also had my eye on a really
cool new pair of sneakers and..."
said Matt.

The inspector couldn't help but
smile.

# ABOUT THE AUTHOR

I love reading and writing thrillers. Nothing beats an exciting story with tons of cliff-hangers and writing *Breathe and You Die* was my chance to work out some amazing stunts and see how my characters coped with the threat of imminent death.

It helps that my son is studying and practising karate. What else do I love? Strong coffee, squash, wild swimming and travelling the world taking photographs, as well as writing books (over 100 up to now). Check out my other books on www.twopeters.com.

# Also in the **RÍVETS** series

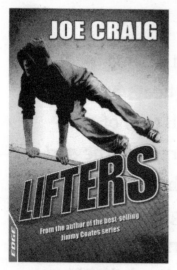

978 1 4451 0555 0 pb
978 1 4451 0850 6 eBook

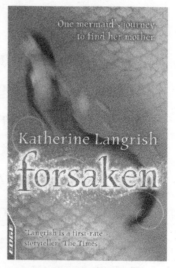

978 1 4451 0557 4 pb
978 1 4451 1073 8 eBook

978 1 4451 0556 7 pb
978 1 4451 0849 0 eBook

978 1 4451 0707 3 pb
978 1 4451 1072 1 eBook